POLAR BEAR PUZZLE

Dear Riley,

We're worried about polar bears, the Arctic's largest predators! Every year they're becoming skinnier, weaker and giving birth to fewer cubs, and scientists aren't sure why.

Aunt Martha, Cousin Alice and I are going to the Arctic town of Churchill, Canada, to get to the bottom of this mystery.

What do you say, Riley—will you "bear" with us?

Uncle Max

ADVENTURES OF RILEY

BY AMANDA LUMRY & LAURA HURWITZ

EaglemonT Press

All photographs by Amanda Lumry except:
pg. 27 caribou herd © Joseph Van Os/Getty Images
pg. 27 caribou © Paul Nicklen/Getty Images
pgs. 28–29 polar bears on ice © Johnny Johnson/Getty Images
pg. 34 global warming map by NASA
pg. 35 "Definitions of the Arctic" map by UNEP/GRID-Arendal Maps and Graphics Library. 2005.
UNEP/GRID-Arendal. 12 Jul 2007 <http://maps.grida.no/go/graphic/definitions_of_the_arctic>

Illustrations and Layouts by Ulkutay & Ulkutay, London WC2E 9RZ
Editing and Digital Compositing by Michael E. Penman

Digital Imaging by Phoenix Color
Printed in China by Phoenix Asia

ISBN-13: 978-1-60040-004-9
ISBN-10: 1-60040-004-3

A special thank you to all the scientists who collaborated on this project. Your time and assistance are very much appreciated.

A portion of the proceeds from your purchase of this licensed product supports the stated educational mission of the Smithsonian Institution – "the increase and diffusion of knowledge." The name of the Smithsonian Institution and the sunburst logo are registered trademarks of the Smithsonian Institution and are registered in the U.S. Patent and Trademark Office.
www.si.edu

2% of the proceeds from this book will be donated to the Wildlife Conservation Society.
http://wcs.org

A royalty of approximately 1% of the retail sales of this book will be received by World Wildlife Fund (WWF) to support their international efforts to protect endangered species and their habitats. ® WWF Registered Trademark. 1986 Panda Symbol © WWF.
www.worldwildlife.org

First edition published 2007 by
Eaglemont Press
PMB 741
15600 NE 8th #B-1
Bellevue, WA 98008
1-877-590-9744
info@eaglemont.com
www.eaglemont.com

Library of Congress Cataloging-in-Publication Data

Lumry, Amanda.
  Polar bear puzzle / by Amanda Lumry & Laura Hurwitz. – 1st ed.
      p. cm. – (Adventures of Riley)
  Summary: Riley, Uncle Max, Aunt Martha, and Cousin Alice meet in northern Canada, where they study and help polar bears that are wandering through towns while waiting for Hudson Bay to freeze over again so that they can hunt for seals.
  ISBN-13: 978-1-60040-004-9 (hardcover : alk. paper)
  ISBN-13: 978-1-60040-005-6 (reinforced lib. bdg. : alk. paper)
  [1. Polar bear–Fiction. 2. Bears–Fiction. 3. Human-animal relationships–Fiction. 4. Zoology–Polar regions–Fiction. 5. Canada–Fiction.] I. Hurwitz, Laura. II. Title.
  PZ7.L9787155Pol 2007
  [Fic]–dc22
                                    2007017589

Riley was so excited! His class was visiting the new polar bear exhibit at the zoo.

"Polar bears are huge!" Riley told his friend Mike. "And look how much they eat!"

"A well-fed bear is a happy bear," said the zookeeper, as she tossed fish after fish to the hungry bears.

I'll have to remember that, thought Riley.

3

A few weeks later, in early November, Riley took a jet to Winnipeg, Canada, and then a small plane into Churchill. He stepped off the plane into a swirling sea of white.

Inside the airport, Alice and Aunt Martha both said, "Welcome to the polar bear capital of the world!"

"But be careful!" said Uncle Max. "There are a lot of hungry polar bears wandering around town looking for food. They've been waiting since the spring thaw for Hudson Bay to freeze over again so they can return to the ice pack to hunt for seals. The bay is usually frozen by now, so the bears are restless. Just yesterday, we had to put three of them in jail."

"Jail?" asked Riley.

"The jail is a pen where we keep polar bears that have broken into houses or garbage cans searching for food," said Aunt Martha. "We give them checkups, tag them and then use a helicopter to drop them back into the wild. By giving checkups to as many bears as possible, we hope to find out what is causing their population to get smaller and weaker."

"Isn't that dangerous?" asked Riley, getting into the bus.

"It's okay," said Alice. "The bears are sound asleep when they're tagged."

6

Later, they switched from their bus to a **tundra buggy** so they could tag polar bears on the way to their Hudson Bay hotel.

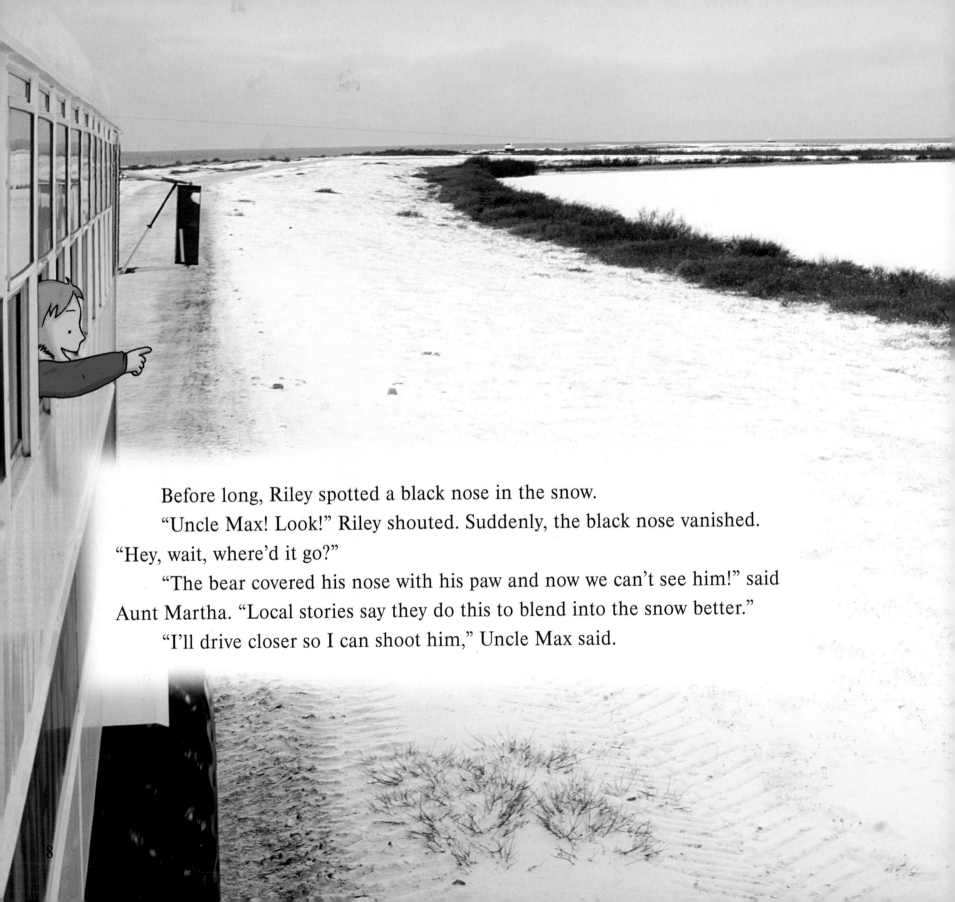

Before long, Riley spotted a black nose in the snow.

"Uncle Max! Look!" Riley shouted. Suddenly, the black nose vanished. "Hey, wait, where'd it go?"

"The bear covered his nose with his paw and now we can't see him!" said Aunt Martha. "Local stories say they do this to blend into the snow better."

"I'll drive closer so I can shoot him," Uncle Max said.

"Shoot?" Riley cried. Uncle Max smiled.

"Don't worry, I'm only using a **tranquilizer** dart. It won't hurt him, and since the medicine in the dart puts him to sleep, he won't hurt us, either. Are you ready for your first patient, Riley?"

Before Riley could answer, Uncle Max's dart hit the bear in the shoulder and the bear went down in a heap.

Tundra

➤ The tundra is a vast, flat, frozen desert found in the polar regions.

➤ The word *tundra* means "treeless" in Finnish.

➤ Below the surface is a layer of soil called permafrost, which stays frozen permanently!

Maxwell "Uncle Max" Plimpton, Professor and Senior Field Biologist

Polar Bear Tagging

Measuring

➤ Using a tape measure, the length and width of the bear are carefully measured and recorded.

➤ The bear is also weighed with a large, heavy-duty scale.

➤ Yearly measurements are used to see if the bear is staying healthy and getting enough to eat.

Scientific Samples

➤ Blood, fat, hair and tissue samples provide valuable information about the bear's health (what it's eating, if it's stored up enough fat for the summer and if it has any diseases).

➤ A small, unneeded tooth is pulled out so it can be viewed under a microscope. The age of the bear can be found by counting the layers of **cementum** on it.

RFID Tagging

➤ A long-range RFID (Radio Frequency Identification) tag is attached to the bear's ear.

➤ With RFID, tagged bears can be identified from a plane or helicopter flying as high as 1,800ft (549m) above the Arctic ice.

➤ This lets scientists learn about the bear's habits, diet and behaviors in a quick, safe and distant manner.

"Alice, are there any other bears around?" asked Uncle Max. She shook her head. "Great. Let's get to work."

"Are you sure this is safe?" Riley asked.

"Positive," said Uncle Max, taking out his tools. With Riley's help, the checkup took less than an hour.

"That's it!" said Aunt Martha. "Now let's get back into the **tundra buggy** before he wakes up!"

Polar Bear

➤ It is the world's largest land carnivore.

➤ Another name for polar bear is *sea bear* or *ice bear*, and it is actually considered a marine mammal.

➤ It has such amazing fur and thick fat that it stays warm even in sub-zero temperatures!

Donald E. Moore, PhD, Associate Director/ Animal Care, National Zoo, Smithsonian Institution

After tagging a few more bears, they arrived at their hotel—a **stationary** "train" made up of connected **tundra buggies**. There were sleeping cars, viewing cars and even a dining car.

"Why do polar bears need the ice to catch seals?" Riley asked at dinner.

"While polar bears are great swimmers, they are slow and clumsy hunters in the open water," said Aunt Martha.

Arctic Hare

➤ Stiff hairs on its hind feet act like snowshoes to support it on the snow.

➤ To help it hide from predators, its hair turns white in the snowy winter and brown in the snow-free summer.

Richard Thorington, Curator of Mammals, National Museum of Natural History, Smithsonian Institution

Arctic Fox

➤ The winter migrations of the arctic fox are longer than any other land-based **mammal**.

➤ An arctic fox eats mostly rodents, such as lemmings, but has been known to feast on dead walruses frozen into the ice.

Linda Gordon, Collection Manager, Division of Mammals, Smithsonian Institution

"They prefer to hunt from the ice, waiting patiently by air holes for seals to come up to breathe. Then the polar bears use their big paws and sharp claws to snatch them from the water," said Uncle Max.

I'm glad I'm not a seal, thought Riley.

Snowy Owl

➤ It spends most of its time **perched** still and silent, looking and listening for prey.

➤ Pairs of snowy owls will defend their nest against all predators, even wolves!

Carter Roberts,
President and CEO,
World Wildlife Fund

The night grew bright as magical green and
white lights began dancing across the sky.
"Riley, it's the northern lights!" cried Alice.
They both watched in wonder.

Northern Lights

➤ The northern lights (scientific name *aurora borealis*) happen when tiny particles from the sun **collide** with gases in Earth's **atmosphere**.

➤ The lights occur most often in late fall and early spring.

➤ While visible on most clear nights in the Arctic, they are seen only every 200 years at the equator.

David Aquilar, Director, Science and Public Programming, Harvard-Smithsonian Center for Astrophysics

In the morning, they took a **tundra buggy** back to Churchill. Hudson Bay still hadn't frozen over, and the polar bears were getting even hungrier.

Ptarmigan

➤ It will burrow under the snow to keep warm.

➤ Its feathers are snow white in winter and brown, gray and white in summer.

➤ Its legs and toes are covered with feathers to keep their feet warm.

Randy Snodgrass, Director, Government Relations, World Wildlife Fund

That night in his new hotel room, Riley dreamed he was surrounded by polar bears. He fed them fish after fish, but still they growled for more.

At breakfast, Riley and Alice found Uncle Max talking to a wildlife management officer.

"These bears need food," said Uncle Max.

"I agree," the officer replied. "Normally, polar bears spend November to June hunting seals from the ice so they can store up enough fat to survive the ice-free months. The rest of the year, they live on the shore and eat almost nothing. No ice means no food."

Ringed Seal

➤ It is the polar bear's main prey.

➤ It is the smallest of the arctic seals, with a maximum weight of 240lbs (108kg).

➤ A mother ringed seal gives birth to babies in a special cave in the ice and snow called a birthing lair, which protects her from bad weather and polar bears.

Charles W. Potter,
Collections Manager,
Marine Mammals, National
Museum of Natural History,
Smithsonian Institution

"I think that's our main problem here," said Uncle Max. "Research shows that the Arctic has been getting warmer than normal in recent years, causing Hudson Bay to freeze later and later. For every week the bay doesn't freeze, adult bears lose about 22 pounds. And when the females don't get enough to eat, they give birth to fewer cubs and aren't able to nurse the cubs they have."

Later that day, Aunt Martha took them on a helicopter tour of Hudson Bay.

"The ice looks like a jigsaw puzzle with a million unconnected pieces," said Riley.

"That's because temperatures have stayed below freezing today," said Uncle Max. "Let's hope this is the beginning of the solid ice pack. In the last 20 years, the Hudson Bay polar bear population has dropped from 1,200 bears to 950 bears. If their hunting season keeps getting shorter because of the warming **climate**, polar bears in the wild could disappear within 100 years."

A well-fed bear is a happy bear, remembered Riley.

"I have an idea," he told Alice.

That evening, Riley and Alice took their leftovers outside. Riley set the napkin of food on the ground and opened it.

GROWWWWL!

It was a POLAR BEAR! Alice screamed. Riley grabbed her hand and they dashed inside their room.

"Maybe feeding the bears wasn't such a good idea after all," said Alice, still shaking.

Riley and Alice were too scared to sleep. They stayed up all night watching out for polar bears. Suddenly, something banged on their door and burst inside! Riley jumped out of bed, while Alice jumped farther in.

Whew! It was just Uncle Max.

"The polar bear jail is overflowing!" Uncle Max cried. "Aunt Martha is making an emergency bear drop, and we need your help!"

At the jail, they saw a polar bear wrapped in a cargo net.

"There are too many bears in town looking for food," said the wildlife officer. "Someone left food out for this one last night."

"That was us," said Riley, turning red. "We thought we were helping."

"Feeding bears is VERY dangerous, and teaching them to rely on humans won't solve their problems," said Uncle Max. "Here comes Aunt Martha now."

"We're sorry." Alice said. "Will the bear be okay?"

"I hope so," said Uncle Max.

25

Caribou

▶ While North Americans call it a caribou, the rest of the world calls it a reindeer!

▶ It regularly digs down through the snow (cratering) to find its favorite food, a lichen known as reindeer moss.

▶ Both the male and female caribou grow antlers.

Joel Berger,
Senior Scientist, Wildlife
Conservation Society

As they flew over the tundra, they watched a herd of caribou through the snowy mist.

Polar Bear

➤ It isn't white! Its skin is black and its hair is actually **pigment**-free and clear. Its fur just appears white when it's clean and in the sunlight.

➤ The North Pole region is the only place to find a polar bear—you won't find one at the South Pole!

➤ While stalking a seal, a polar bear will place each paw softly on the snow to keep from scaring away its prey with a crunch.

Robert Buchanan, President,
Polar Bears International

"Look! The bay has frozen over! I can see bears walking on it!" said Riley.

"Just in time," said Uncle Max.

Aunt Martha landed near the edge of the bay. Everyone jumped into action. Riley and Alice watched for other polar bears while Aunt Martha unhooked the net and Uncle Max loosened the straps. The bear began to stir.

"We have to free him quickly!" said Uncle Max.

"The net is stuck on his ear!" Alice cried.

"It's also caught on his back paw!" shouted Riley.

"Careful!" warned Uncle Max. Riley's heart was pounding as he lifted the net over the bear's sharp claws. The bear growled softly just as Riley got him loose.

"Great job, Carrot Top!" said Uncle Max. "Now let's go!"

31

As the helicopter lifted off, they watched as the bear stood up and moved slowly onto the newly frozen seawater.

"We did it!" said Alice.

"Hopefully this bear will be eating seal for supper," said Aunt Martha.

"You guys were great," said Uncle Max. "Thankfully, the ice froze today, and the bears will survive another year. But **climate** change is still a big problem for polar bears, and with Arctic temperatures rising twice as fast as the rest of the world, they are still at great risk."

Climate Change

➤ Earth has warmed about 1.44°F (0.8°C) in the last 200 years due to the carbon dioxide gas created by burning **fossil fuels** and other activities like deforestation.

➤ This warming is affecting **ecosystems** around the planet, from the poles to the equator, and from coral reefs to the highest mountaintops.

➤ If warming continues, by the year 2080 there will be no ice in Hudson Bay at all.

Lara Hansen, Chief Climate Change Scientist, World Wildlife Fund

Riley thought about that all the way back to Churchill.

"It doesn't sound like there is much hope," he said.

"If everyone works together to help stop rising temperatures, polar bears have a chance. By doing simple things such as recycling and using less energy, we can reduce the amount of human-made pollution, such as carbon dioxide, that traps heat in the **atmosphere**," said Aunt Martha.

"That would sure make life in the Arctic more *bear-able*!" added Riley.

33

Back home, Riley told everyone about polar bear jail, polar bear air drops and the northern lights. He talked to his class about saving energy, and together, they started a recycling program.

Riley returned to living the life of a nine-year-old, until he once again got a letter from his Uncle Max.

Where will Riley go next?

FURTHER INFORMATION

North America

Canada

Nunavut

Hudson Bay

Churchill

Manitoba

Ontario

Quebec

Glossary:

atmosphere: the gases surrounding a planet

cementum: a thin layer of bone deposited in a polar bear's teeth every year

climate: the weather in an area over a long time

collide: to hit hard when moving

ecosystems: areas where plants, animals and the environment interact together

fossil fuels: fuels such as coal, oil or gas formed in the past from the remains of living things

mammal: a warm-blooded creature with a spine, fed by milk from its mother

perched: sat or rested on something

pigment: the natural coloring of animal or plant tissue

stationary: not moving

tranquilizer: a medicine that causes deep sleep

tundra buggy: a bus-like vehicle with large tires used to drive easily and safely across Arctic tundra

Carbon Footprint

➤ A footprint shows how much space you take up. A carbon footprint is how much carbon dioxide (CO_2) a person makes.

➤ Using energy like electricity, gas or oil causes CO_2 to be put into the air.

➤ CO_2 is also created in the process of making food, clothing and most other products people use.

➤ Cars produce about 1lb of CO_2 per mile (1kg per 3.5km).

➤ Per person per year, Americans produce CO_2 equal to the weight of four African elephants.

➤ CO_2 causes higher temperatures. This makes ice melt at the poles.

Bert Drake, Plant Physiologist, Environmental Research Center, Smithsonian Institution

What is the Arctic? The Arctic consists of the Arctic Ocean at the North Pole, which is surrounded by continents and islands. The central Arctic Ocean is frozen year-round, while the southern limit of the Arctic region is defined in many ways:

High Arctic	----- Arctic Circle
Low Arctic	—— Treeline
Sub-Arctic	—— 10˚C July Isotherm—Where average summer temperatures don't rise above 10˚C (50˚F).
Transition zone from Temperate sub-Arctic to High Arctic	

Pacific Ocean

Alaska

Canada

Magnetic North Pole

Arctic Ocean

Geographic North Pole

Russia

Greenland

Atlantic Ocean